Georgetown Elementary School
Indian Prairie School District
Aurora, Illinois

Little Raccoon

Little Raccoon

by **Lilian Moore**

illustrated by **Doug Cushman**

An Early Chapter Book
Henry Holt and Company
New York

For Jazmin, who grew up
with Little Raccoon
—L. M.

To Rick and Pat, and the
landscape in the Warners
—D. C.

Henry Holt and Company, LLC, *Publishers since 1866*
115 West 18th Street, New York, New York 10011
www.henryholt.com

Henry Holt is a registered trademark of Henry Holt and Company, LLC
Little Raccoon and the Thing in the Pool text copyright © 1963 by Lilian Moore
Little Raccoon and the Outside World text copyright © 1965 by Lilian Moore
Little Raccoon and No Trouble at All text copyright © 1972 by Lilian Moore
Text compilation copyright © 2002 by Lilian Moore
Illustrations copyright © 2002 by Doug Cushman / All rights reserved.
Distributed in Canada by H. B. Fenn and Company Ltd.
The Little Raccoon books were first published as
separate editions in the United States by McGraw-Hill.

Library of Congress Cataloging-in-Publication Data
Moore, Lilian.
Little Raccoon / by Lilian Moore; illustrated by Doug Cushman.
Summary: Little Raccoon has adventures fishing by himself at night, venturing
into the outside world beyond his woods, and babysitting two tricky chipmunks.
[1. Raccoons—Fiction. 2. Animals—Fiction.] I. Cushman, Doug, ill. II. Title.
PZ7.M7865 Lh 2001   [Fic]—dc21   00-40981

ISBN 0-8050-6543-1 / First Henry Holt Edition—2002
Printed in the United States of America on acid-free paper. ∞
1   3   5   7   9   10   8   6   4   2

Contents

The Thing
in the Pool

Little Raccoon was little, but he was brave.

Once day Mother Raccoon said, "Tonight the moon will be bright and full. Can you go to the running stream all by yourself, Little Raccoon? Can you bring back some crayfish for supper?"

"Oh yes, yes!" said Little Raccoon. "I'll bring back the best crayfish you ever ate!"

Little Raccoon was little, but he *was* brave.

That night the moon came up big and full and very bright.

"Go now, Little Raccoon," said his mother. "Walk till you come to the pool. You will see a big tree lying across the pool. Walk across the pool on the tree. The best place to dig for crayfish is on the other side."

Little Raccoon went off in the bright moonlight. He was so happy and so proud. Here he was—walking in the woods all by himself for the very first time!

He walked a little. He ran a little. And now and then he skipped.

Soon Little Raccoon came to the place where the tall trees grew. There was Old Porcupine, resting. He was surprised to see Little Raccoon walking in the woods without his mother.

"Where are you going, all by yourself?" asked Old Porcupine.

"To the running stream," said Little Raccoon proudly. "I'm going to get some crayfish for supper."

"Be careful, Little Raccoon," said Old Porcupine. "You don't have what I have, you know!"

"I'm not afraid," said Little Raccoon. He was little, but he was brave.

Little Raccoon went on in the bright moonlight.

He walked a little. He ran a little. And now and then he skipped.

Soon he came to the place where the sweet grass grew. There was Big Skunk. He was surprised, too, to see Little Raccoon walking in the woods without his mother.

"Where are you going, all by yourself?" asked Big Skunk.

"To the running stream," said Little Raccoon proudly. "I'm going to get some crayfish for supper."

"Be careful, Little Raccoon," said Big Skunk. "You don't have what I have, you know!"

"I'm not afraid," said Little Raccoon, and he went on.

Not far from the running stream he saw Fat Rabbit. Fat Rabbit was sleeping, but he opened one eye. Then he jumped up.

"My, you scared me!" he said. "Where are you going, Little Raccoon, all by yourself?"

"I'm going to the running stream," said Little Raccoon proudly. "Way over there on the other side of the pool."

"OOOOOH!" said Fat Rabbit. "Aren't you afraid of IT?"

"Afraid of what?" asked Little Raccoon.

"Of the thing in the pool!" said Fat Rabbit. "I am!"

"Well, I'm not!" said Little Raccoon, and he went on.

Soon Little Raccoon came to the big tree that was lying across the pool.

"This is where I cross," said Little Raccoon to himself. "And over there on the other side is where I dig for crayfish."

Little Raccoon walked onto the tree, and began to cross the pool. He *was* brave, but he did wish he had not met Fat Rabbit. He did not want to think about IT. He did not want to think about the thing in the pool. But he couldn't help it. He just had to stop—and look.

There *was* something in the pool! There it

was, in the bright moonlight, looking up at him!

Little Raccoon did not want to show he was afraid. So he made a face.

The thing in the pool made a face, too. And what a mean face it was!

Little Raccoon turned and ran. He ran past Fat Rabbit so fast he scared him again.

He ran and ran and did not stop till he saw Big Skunk.

"What is it? What is it?" asked Big Skunk.

"There's a big thing in the pool!" said Little Raccoon. "I can't get past it!"

"Do you want me to go with you?" asked Big Skunk. "I can make it go away."

"Oh no, no!" said Little Raccoon quickly. "You don't have to do that!"

"Well, then," said Big Skunk, "take a stone with you. Just show that thing in the pool you have a stone!"

Little Raccoon did want to bring home the crayfish. So he took a stone, and he walked back to the pool.

"Maybe the thing went away," Little Raccoon said to himself.

But no. When he looked down into the water, there it was. Little Raccoon did not want to show he was afraid. He held up his stone. But the thing in the pool held up a stone, too. And what a big stone it was! Little Raccoon was brave, but he *was* little.

He ran like anything. He ran and ran and he did not stop till he saw Old Porcupine.

"What is it? What is it?" asked Old Porcupine.

Little Raccoon told him about the thing in the pool.

"He had a stone, too," said Little Raccoon. "A big, BIG stone!"

"Then you must have a stick this time," said Old Porcupine. "Go back and show that you have big stick!"

Little Raccoon did want to bring home the crayfish. So he took a stick and walked back to the pool.

"Maybe this time it went away," Little Raccoon said to himself.

But no. The thing in the pool was still there. Little Raccoon did not wait. He held up his big stick and shook it. But the thing in

the pool had a stick, too. A big, BIG stick. And
it shook the stick at Little Raccoon.

Little Raccoon dropped his stick and ran.

He ran and ran
   past Fat Rabbit—
      past Big Skunk—
         past Old Porcupine—
and he did not stop till he was home.

Little Raccoon told his mother all about the thing in the pool.

"Oh, Mother," he said, "I wanted to go for crayfish all by myself. I wanted to bring home our supper!"

"And you shall!" said Mother Raccoon. "Go back to the pool, Little Raccoon. But this time do not make a face. Do not carry a stone. Do not carry a stick."

"But what *shall* I do?" asked Little Raccoon.

"Just smile," said Mother Raccoon. "This time just smile at the thing in the pool."

"Is that all?" asked Little Raccoon. "Are you sure?"

"That is all," said his mother. "I am sure."

Little Raccoon was brave and his mother was sure. So he went all the way back to the pool again.

"Maybe the thing went away at last," he said to himself.

But no. There it was! Little Raccoon made himself stand still. He made himself look down into the water. Then he made himself smile at the thing in the pool. The thing in the pool smiled back! Little Raccoon was so happy he began to laugh. The thing in the pool seemed to laugh, too, just like a happy raccoon.

"Now it wants to be friends," said Little Raccoon to himself. "Now I can cross!" And he ran along the tree to the other side of the pool. There in the running stream, Little Raccoon began to dig. Soon he had all the crayfish he could carry.

He ran back along the tree across the pool.
This time Little Raccoon waved to the thing in
the pool. The thing in the pool waved back!

Little Raccoon went home with the crayfish as fast as he could go. It was the best crayfish he and Mother Raccoon ever ate. Mother Raccoon said so, too.

"I can go by myself anytime now," said Little Raccoon. "I'm not afraid of the thing in the pool now."

"I know," said Mother Raccoon.

"The thing in the pool isn't mean at all!" said Little Raccoon.

"I know," said Mother Raccoon.

Little Raccoon looked at his mother. "Tell me," he said. "What *is* the thing in the pool?"

Mother Raccoon began to laugh. Then she told him.

The Outside World

Little Raccoon looked out at the woods around him. There was nothing to see but the woods. Nothing but green woodland all around. Little Raccoon sat thinking.

"Mother," he asked, "do the woods have an end? Do they go on and on—or do they end?"

"The woods have an end," said his mother. "Past the running stream, past the bright berry bushes, past the open grass where the young oak stands—the woods end."

"But what is there—after the woods end?" asked Little Raccoon.

"The outside world," said Mother Raccoon.

"The outside world!" cried Little Raccoon. "What is it like?"

"It's too hard to explain," said his mother. "Why don't you run out and play?"

Little Raccoon ran out, but he did not play. He sat down to think.

Mother Skunk came by with her little ones. Little Raccoon jumped up and ran to her.

"Please!" he said. "What is it like in the outside world?"

"Way out there?" said Mother Skunk. "Past the running stream, past the bright berry bushes, past the open grass where the young oak stands?"

"Yes! Yes!" cried Little Raccoon.

"It's too hard to explain," said Mother Skunk. And she went in to visit Mother Raccoon.

The little skunks wanted to play, but Little Raccoon wanted to think. So the little skunks sat down to think, too.

"If I go to the running stream," said Little Raccoon, "I can catch a crayfish. I can stand on a big rock. And maybe I can *see* the outside world!"

"Oh good!" cried the skunks. "We will go, too. Maybe we can catch a frog!"

Little Raccoon looked at the skunks. "Well, come along," he said. "But stay right behind me, and do as I say."

Off they went to the running stream, and the little skunks stayed right behind Little Raccoon, all the way.

Little Raccoon looked for crayfish.

The little skunks looked for a frog. They saw a frog, and they ran after it. But the little skunks bumped heads, and the frog got away.

Little Raccoon did catch a crayfish. Then he got up on a big rock. But he did not see the outside world.

"If I go on to the berry bushes," said Little Raccoon, "I can eat some berries. I can climb a tall bush. And maybe then I can see the outside world."

"We *love* berries!" said the skunks.

"Well, come along then," said Little Raccoon. "But stay right behind me, and do as I say."

Off they went to the berry bushes, and the little skunks stayed right behind Little Raccoon.

They ate and ate the fat bright berries. One more. And one more. And one more.

Then Little Raccoon climbed a tall bush. But he did not see the outside world.

"If I go on to the open grass," he said, "I can catch some bugs and creeping things. I can climb the young oak tree. Maybe then I can see the outside world."

"We just *love* bugs and creeping things!" cried the little skunks.

"Come along," said Little Raccoon, and on they went to the open grass.

33

They ran after bugs and creeping things,
and they ate and ate.

Then Little Raccoon climbed up the young
oak tree. And he *did* see something.

"That's it!" cried Little Raccoon. "That must be the outside world!"

"What is it? What is it like?" asked the skunks.

"I am going to find out," said Little Raccoon.

"Oh good!" cried the skunks. "We will go, too!"

This time Little Raccoon said no. "You are too little," he said. "You stay here. I will come back and tell you."

Little Raccoon ran across the open grass
at the end of the woods. Then he stopped
and looked around.

What was this? Maybe it was like the tree over the pool in the woods. Maybe it was something to run across.

Little Raccoon ran across. *Bump!*

He ran back. *Bump!*

He jumped off quickly. It was *not* like the tree over the pool.

Then Little Raccoon smelled something. All good things were mixed up into that one good smell! *Sniff! Sniff!* It came from here. Little Raccoon looked inside. So many good things!

One thing was best of all. But it *was* a little hard to eat.

Little Raccoon ran back to the skunks. He ran back to tell them about the thing that went *bump*, and the good smell, and the long, long, *long* things to eat.

"You stay right here," said Little Raccoon. "I will come back and tell you more."

Little Raccoon ran across the grass again to the end of the woods. He looked around. What was this?

It must be a tree. But what BIG leaves it had! It was hard to climb, too.

Little Raccoon ran to the fence. Then he jumped from the fence to the tree.

The tree began to go around! Little Raccoon wanted to get off. He jumped again, and there he was, sitting right in one of the BIG leaves!

At last
Little Raccoon
got off. He ran back to the
skunks to tell them about the trees
in the outside world.

"They have big, big leaves," said Little Raccoon. "And guess what! The trees go around and around!"

"We will stay right here," said the little skunks quickly. "You can come back and tell us more."

Again Little Raccoon ran across the grass at the end of the woods.

Again he stopped and looked around. What was this?

Little Raccoon ran over to see.

There was something to open. Little Raccoon opened it.

There was something to pull. Little Raccoon pulled it.

Whoosh! Down came the water. Cold water. Then warm water. Then HOT water.

"OW!" cried Little Raccoon, and he jumped out quickly. Little Raccoon ran all the way back to the little skunks.

"Guess what!" he cried. "The outside world is where they keep the rain! I turned on the rain! And guess what! It was hot rain!"

"Hot rain!" cried the little skunks. "We want to go home!"

So did Little Raccoon. He had so *many* things to tell his mother!

"Come along!" he cried to the little skunks.

They ran back across the open grass. And they did not stop for one little bug. They ran past the berry bushes. And they did not stop for one fat bright berry. They ran past the running stream. And they did not stop to look for a crayfish or a frog. They ran all the way back—all the way to Little Raccoon's house. Mother Skunk was still visiting with Mother Raccoon.

"Guess what!" cried the little skunks. "We went all the way to the open grass, and Little Raccoon went to see the outside world!"

"The outside world!" said Mother Skunk. "Think of that!"

"Did you really?" said Mother Raccoon. "What was it like, Little Raccoon?"

What was it like? Little Raccoon began to think—about things that went *bump!* if you ran across, about long, *long* things to eat, about trees that went around, about rain that was *hot*.

"It's too hard to explain," said Little Raccoon.

No Trouble at All

"Little Raccoon," said his mother, "will you help?"

Little Raccoon jumped up. "Do you want me to go to the running stream?"

"No," said his mother.

"Do you want me to get some crayfish for supper?"

"No," said his mother. "I want you to listen. Mother Chipmunk and I must go to the outside world. Will you take care of her baby chipmunks till we get back?"

"Will you, Little Raccoon?" asked Mother Chipmunk.

Little Raccoon looked at the baby chipmunks. "I never did *that* before," he said.

The two chipmunks sat very still, looking up at Little Raccoon.

"See how good they are," said Mother Chipmunk. "They will be no trouble at all."

So little. So good. And no trouble at all.

"All right," said Little Raccoon. "I will take care of them."

"Thank you, Little Raccoon," said Mother Chipmunk.

Mother Raccoon thanked him, too. And they went away.

Little Raccoon stood looking at the baby chipmunks.

"He's my brother," said one.

"She's my sister," said the other.

"Oh," said Little Raccoon.

The chipmunks sat looking at Little Raccoon.

"Play with us," said the brother.

"Play follow me," said the sister.

"I never did *that* before," said Little Raccoon.

"All you do is follow us," said the brother. The chipmunks ran to a tree.

"Come on!" they cried. "Follow us!" And they ran up the tree.

Little Raccoon ran up the tree, too.

One chipmunk ran out on a branch. *Whoosh!* He jumped into the next tree.

"Follow me!" he cried.

The other chipmunk ran out on the branch, too. *Whoosh!* She jumped into the next tree. "Follow me!" she cried.

Little Raccoon ran out on the branch, too. But the branch was too small for him. *Crash!* He came tumbling down.

"Follow us!" cried the chipmunks. And they ran to the old stone wall. There was a hole in the wall, and one chipmunk ran inside.

The other called, "Follow me!" And he ran into the hole, too.

Little Raccoon picked himself up and went over to the wall. "This game is hard work," he thought.

"Come in! Follow us!" called the chipmunks.

Little Raccoon stuck his head into the hole. Then he put his front paws in. But the hole was too small for him. "I can't get in," he said. He pushed with his back paws. "I can't get out!" he cried.

"Little Raccoon is stuck," said the brother chipmunk.

"You look funny," said the sister. And they began to laugh.

Little Raccoon did not think it was funny. He began to wiggle. This way and that. And he pushed and pushed. At last with a wiggle and a push, he came tumbling out.

The chipmunks ran out of the hole. "Here we are!" they cried.

"No more games!" said Little Raccoon. "You sit here, and you sit there." The little chipmunks sat very still, looking up at Little Raccoon.

"Do you know any tricks?" asked the brother.

"No," said Little Raccoon.

"We know a good one," said the sister. "Can we show you?"

"What's the trick?" asked Little Raccoon.

"We can hide behind a tree so that you *never* see us," said the brother.

"Never!" said the sister.

"But all I have to do is go around the tree," said Little Raccoon.

"Try it," said the brother. And the chipmunks hid behind a tree.

Little Raccoon went around the tree, but the chipmunks went faster. He did not see them. "Are you there?" he asked.

"Yes!" cried the chipmunks.

Little Raccoon went around the tree again. Around and around. To his surprise, he still did not see the chipmunks. He went faster and faster. Around and around.

All at once the world was going around

and around, faster and faster. Little Raccoon was so dizzy he had to sit down.

"Here we are!" cried the chipmunks.

"No more tricks," said Little Raccoon. "You sit here, and you sit there!"

The little chipmunks sat very still, looking up at Little Raccoon. "I'm hungry," said the sister.

"So am I," said the brother.

"And so am I!" thought Little Raccoon. He looked at the baby chipmunks.

"Do you like crayfish?" he asked.

"We like butternuts and beechnuts," said the brother.

"And hazelnuts and hickory nuts," said the sister. "What's crayfish?"

"It's the best of all!" said Little Raccoon. "Let's go to the running stream and get some."

The chipmunks jumped up.

"Stay right behind me!" said Little Raccoon. And off they went.

On the way, Little Raccoon thought about crayfish. "Ah! Crayfish!"

He began to sing:

"Ah! Crayfish! Crayfish!
It's an eat-it-every-day fish."

And he sang it again and again.

Soon he saw Old Porcupine, resting by a tree.

"Hello, Little Raccoon," said Old Porcupine. "Where are you going all by yourself?"

"All by myself?" said Little Raccoon. And he turned around to look. "Oh, *no!*"

"What is it?" asked Old Porcupine

"I've lost some chipmunks," said Little Raccoon.

Just then something hit Little Raccoon on the head.

"Here I am," the brother chipmunk called from a tree.

Something hit Little Raccoon on the head again.

"Here I am!" called the sister chipmunk.

"Come down!" said Little Raccoon. "Come right down!"

The baby chipmunks came running down from the tree. "Here we are!" they cried.

Little Raccoon looked at them. "I must do something," he thought. "I must do

something to make them behave."
But all he said was "Follow me."

And they went on to the running stream.
Up the stream was the beaver pond. And
there was Beaver, working on his house in
the middle of the pond.

Little Raccoon looked at Beaver. "I must
do something," he thought, "and I know
what it is!"

Little Raccoon began to fish. The chipmunks sat and looked at him. They saw him catch a fine, fat crayfish. They saw him jump into the water and swim out to Beaver's house. Little Raccoon sat there and ate the crayfish.

"Oh," he called to the chipmunks, "This crayfish is *so* good!"

"We want some!" said the chipmunks. "We want some!"

"Beaver," said Little Raccoon, "the chipmunks want to come out here. Will you give them a ride?"

"Hop on!" said Beaver to the chipmunks. And he took them to Little Raccoon.

"You sit here," said Little Raccoon, "and you sit there." And he gave them some crayfish. Then Little Raccoon jumped into the water and swam back across the pond. He began to fish again, and soon he had a fine, fat crayfish.

The little chipmunks looked across the pond at Little Raccoon. "We don't like crayfish," said the brother.

"We *hate* crayfish," said the sister.

Little Raccoon went on eating.

"We don't like it here," said the brother. "We don't like it at *all.*"

Little Raccoon went on eating.

"We want to go home!" said the brother.

"Little Raccoon," cried the sister, "we want to go home."

Little Raccoon looked across the pond at the chipmunks. "No more games?" he said.

"No," said the chipmunks.

"No more tricks?"

"No," said the chipmunks.

"No more tree fun?"

"Oh no!" said the chipmunks.

"Beaver," said Little Raccoon, "the chipmunks want to come back."

"Hop on!" said Beaver to the chipmunks. And he took them back across the pond.

"Stay right behind me," said Little Raccoon. "All the way home!"

That's what the chipmunks did. And all the way home, Little Raccoon sang:

"Ah! Crayfish! Crayfish!
It's an eat-it-every-day fish."

They got home just as Mother Raccoon and Mother Chipmunk did.

"Hello, my little ones," said Mother Chipmunk. "Were you good? Were they good, Little Raccoon?"

The chipmunks looked at Little Raccoon.

Little Raccoon looked at the chipmunks.

"No trouble at all," said Little Raccoon.